Secret of the Dance

story by Andrea Spalding *and* Alfred Scow

illustrations by Darlene Gait

Orca Book Publishers

For Ethan, who loves to dance.
—Andrea Spalding

In loving memory of my mother, Tle'La'Wick, Alice Scow.
—Alfred Scow

I would like to dedicate this book to all the Native Baha'is in Canada, who make it possible to forgive and grow, as the creator intended. May we all one day unite, and discover home within our own hearts—once again...
—Darlene Gait

Many years ago, when the world and I were younger, my family defied the government.

"Dancing's against the law," announced the Indian Agent.
"We need to hold a Potlatch ceremony," whispered the Elders.
We were sent out to play.

West Wind

“The salmon are running,” explained the Elders. “We should follow.”

We helped pack the boat with food and clothing, everything needed for a fishing trip.

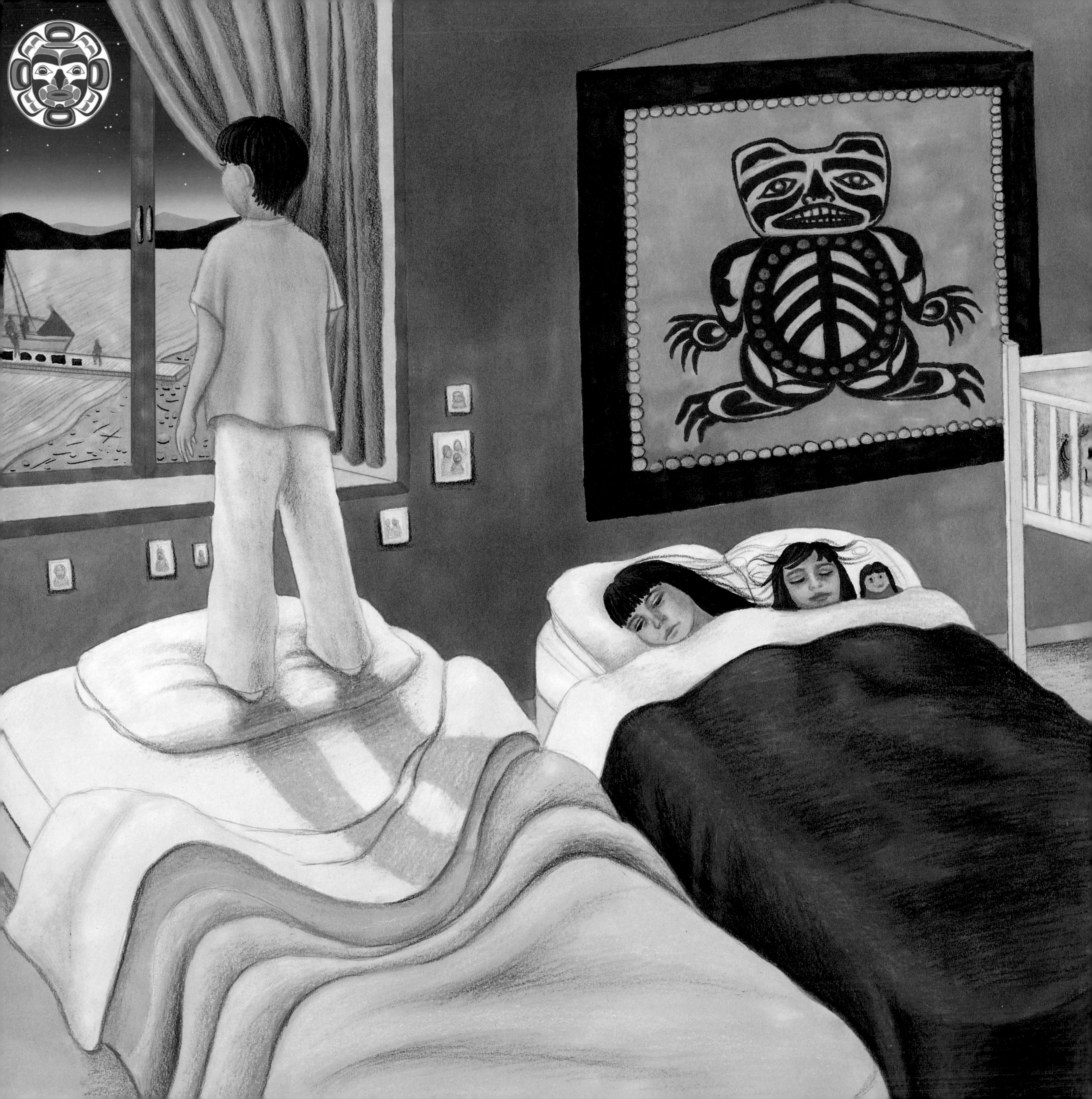

“Sleep,” said Mother. “Dawn will come early.”

G’naa, the baby, slept. My sisters, Tlakwetl and Whahta, slept. I was too excited.

That night, I heard noises outside. I peeked as strangely shaped, blanket-wrapped parcels were hidden in the boat.

"Watl'kina, help your grandmother into the boat," called Father.

"Careful, Ga'Gaas," I said as I steadied her arm.

The boat rocked, and Ga'Gaas sat down hard.

"Oops." I bit my lip.

She chuckled and patted my cheek. The young ones cuddled up beside her.

We waved to the Indian Agent.

*Putt…putt…putt…putt….*The fish boat sailed through the dawn light.

Beyond the islands, the wind was fresh and the waves danced.

Mother gave us dried berries and smoked eulachon, a special treat.

We sailed all day through sun, wind and showers. When we became restless, Ga'Gaas told stories, tales about our Bear Clan, of the Hamatsa and the Dzunukwa, the Wild Woman who kidnapped children.

Dolphins leapt, Eagles soared and passing Orcas spouted.

"See the Max'inuxw? We have their blessing," said Ga'Gaas.

Father scanned the ocean.

No government boats were following.

Ja'Qwa

“Your eyes are young and sharp, Watl’kina. Watch for the inlet,” said Father. “We must not miss the entrance.”

I knelt in the prow and stared and stared at the coastline. “I see it!” I yelled.

Father smiled and turned the wheel.

“Ghi’lakas’la,” shouted the watchers posted at the entrance. “Welcome!”

“Ghi’lakas’la,” we called. Our voices echoed along the cliffs.

The inlet narrowed. The mountains were the highest I’d seen.

Our fish boat seemed very small.

It was almost evening when we came to the village huddling between the forest and the shore. We anchored in the river.

Our relatives fetched us in a canoe.

I was glad to run and stretch my legs on shore.

“Time for bed,” said Mother.

“We’re not tired,” we protested.

Mother took me to one side. “We need your help, Watl’kina. Father and I must join the Elders. The children should not come in case the Indian Agent followed us. There may be trouble.”

I nodded.

Mother drew the curtains and tucked us into bed.

My throat ached with disappointment.

We watched through the gap between the curtains.

Shadowy figures carried the blanket parcels from the boats to the Gookji, the Big House.

We listened, but heard only a low murmur of voices, the wind in the cedars and the waves on the shore.

G'naa and Tlakwetl fell asleep.

Whahta cried, "I want to go to the feast!" She tried to get out of bed.

"Be good," I said, "or the Dzunukwa will get you."

I repeated Grandmother's story.

The drumming and singing began before I finished, but Whahta's eyes were drooping so I dared not stop.

Finally they all slept.

I crept to the window and lifted the curtain.

The village was dark. Even the dogs were silent. But the drums made the air vibrate. The singing grew louder.

It was more than I could stand.

I crept out into the night.

"Aiii, Aiii hooooo," chanted voices.

DAA, ta ta ta. DAA, ta ta ta, called the drums.

My feet tapped in response, and I followed the sound, dancing alone down the village street.

Suddenly I heard rustlings and movement.

Strange masked figures surrounded me.

Ga'Gaas' stories had come to life. Eagle, Whale, Raven, Bear, Wolf, even Dzunukwa, the Wild Woman, towered over me.

I turned to run.

The Wild Woman grasped my shoulder. My knees trembled.

"It is good you see us," murmured Dzunukwa, "for this may be the last time we dance. Watch for the Hamatsa."

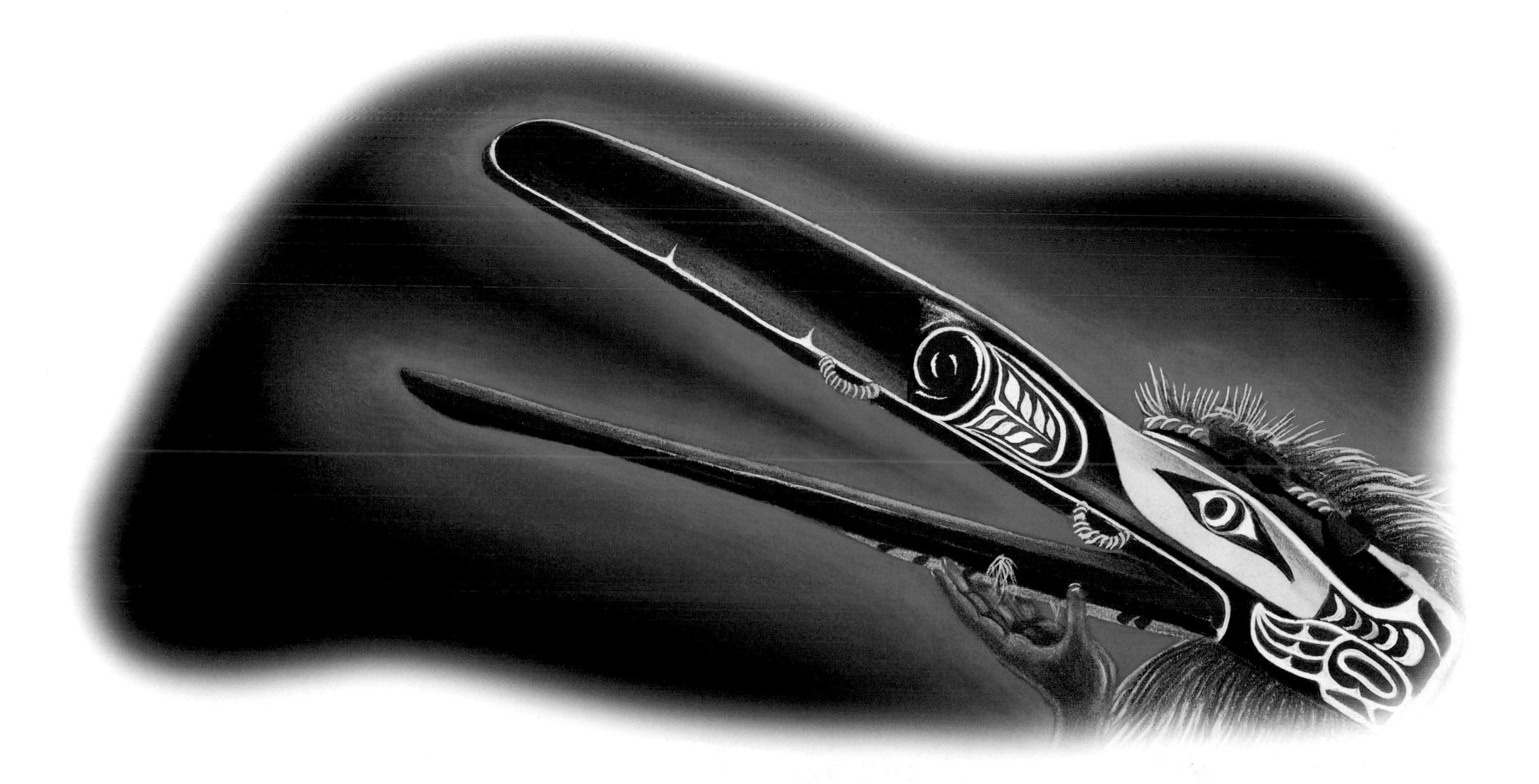

The drums called again, and the doors were flung open. The figures left me to enter the Big House.

I darted between the closing doors and hid in the shadows.

Fire was the only light. It glinted on the button blankets and masks as the dancers circled, weaving in and out of the smoke.

I saw Bear, my clan symbol. He passed right by me. I could not mistake his sharp claws and fierce white teeth. In the firelight he was a real bear, called onto the floor to dance his story.

The Hamatsa appeared from behind the screen.

He danced in and out of the shadows.

There was something familiar about him. Something in the way he moved and proudly held his head.

I stared, but the flames flickered. I could not see his face.

The Hamatsa danced beyond the fire. A log cracked and flared. For a brief moment the shadows were banished.

I knew him.

That was the only time I ever saw my father dance.

Before the dancers finished, I sneaked back to bed.
My parents and I never spoke of that night.
The masks were re-wrapped in blankets and hidden from the authorities for many years.

Now I am older than my father was when he danced. Each time I step in procession and wear the regalia forbidden him, I rejoice. Tears cloud my eyes as I watch the dancers. For now the government invites us to dance, to honor visiting kings and queens and other guests.

Life makes strange circles.

Hehmaas. That is everything.

Historical Note

This story is fiction but is based on an incident in the life of the child Watl'kina, now known as retired judge Alfred Scow, Elder of the Kwick'wa'sut'eneuk, one of the Kwakwa'ka'wakw Nations.

Alfred was born in Alert Bay in 1927.

In 1885 the Canadian government passed a law forbidding Aboriginal people to hold ceremonials, including the Potlatch. But these ceremonies were the very essence of Aboriginal culture and so were continued in secrecy. After World War I, the government made determined efforts to stop the ceremonies by raiding Potlatches. Once caught, the participants were given a choice between prison and having their masks and other ceremonial regalia confiscated. In 1922, Alfred's grandfather Chief John Scow and two brothers served time in prison rather than give up the family's masks and regalia.

In 1935, Alfred's family sailed from Gilford Island to the village of Kingcome at the head of Kingcome Inlet. There, a branch of the Scow family hosted a forbidden Potlatch as a memorial for Alfred's grandfather.

Alfred and his sisters were told they couldn't attend. If the Potlatch had been raided, any children found there would have been removed from their parents' care. Alfred sneaked inside to see his father dance. Luckily, the officials did not discover them that night.

Many of Alert Bay's masks were confiscated in 1921 and only returned to the people of the Kwakwa'ka'wakw Nations in 1979. They are now on public display in Alert Bay's U'mista Cultural Center. They watch from the walls as the traditional dances are taught to today's children.

Canada's Potlatch law was finally repealed in 1951.